THE HOLIDAY SWAP

MELISSA HILL

THE HOLIDAY SWAP

A FESTIVE NOVELLA

CHAPTER 1

*I*t was unbelievable how a couple of snow flurries could make everyone in Boston suddenly forget how to drive, Ally Walker mused, frustrated as she sat in the back of the taxi winging its way to the airport.

Granted, it wasn't often they made it all the way till December without any significant accumulations.

But none of that especially mattered right now. All she could think about was making her flight.

"Outta the way!" her cab driver remonstrated as the car in front stopped suddenly at the airport terminal's no stopping zone.

Ally scooted towards the edge of the back

seat in an attempt to see out of the windshield. "You know what … this is good. I can walk the rest of the way."

The driver pulled up to the curb, and tapping her phone to pay him, (adding a nice holiday tip) she exited the car quickly and hopped round back to grab her stuff from the trunk. Extending the pull handle of her carry-on suitcase, she was off and running into the terminal building, not even letting her three inch pumps slow her down.

Using her free hand to pull her trench coat tighter around her body and her wool sheath dress, Ally attempted to create a barrier against the bitter cold. And questioned what she could have been thinking this morning not wearing pantyhose while bitter snow flurries pelted her bare legs.

Inside, she made it to the security line in quick time. After years of practice, Ally could do this in her sleep. Which was fortunate because after a non-stop work day that began at 5am this morning, she *felt* half asleep.

"Come on, come on," she muttered impatiently as she waited for the airline app to load so she could pull up her digital boarding pass.

But with 'no reservation found' displaying onscreen, Ally reluctantly gave up her place in the line to call her assistant.

"Walters Tech," Mel answered, in her most professional and chipper voice.

"It's me," Ally greeted, trying not to make herself sound too demanding, but time was of the essence. "Why can't I check in for my flight?"

"You know you're not with your usual, right? They don't fly into your friend's location. I thought I'd mentioned that. "

Ally winced. She hated changes of plan.

"I didn't know that. Text me the info? Maybe if I run to the gate I can still make it."

"Yeah you're cutting it kinda close, considering..."

"I had to make a stop by my apartment on the way," Ally explained, glancing at the garment bag laid carefully on top of her luggage, sequins sparkling brightly through the plastic covering.

She'd fallen instantly in love with the dress nearly four years ago when she happened to pass by it in a department store window and threw caution to the wind, purchasing it without any particular occasion in mind.

Since then the gown had been sitting in her closet, just waiting for the right moment to shine. And in her suitcase was a gorgeous pair of silver heels with jewelled straps she'd purchased a week later to match.

Just in case an opportunity presented itself, which it seemed would happen this weekend, courtesy of Ally's best friend Lara's invite to the Snow Ball, a gala event being held in her Maine hometown.

A girl couldn't just wear any old shoes with *that* dress.

Ally hadn't put much else thought into packing for this particular visit though, since her friend had more clothes than Saks and she and Lara were pretty much the same size.

Lara's was by all accounts a *very* small town, so she figured most other outings while there would call for a pretty casual dress code.

Besides, the visit was just a short festive diversion from her final destination; Florida, which called for shorts, bikinis and not a whole lot else.

Ally always preferred to travel light.

"You wouldn't *believe* how crowded the airport is today," she muttered to Mel now.

Ally had flown over 100,000 miles that year, and never had to fight her way through this many people. All of them just taking their time, walking in large groups, talking, laughing, carrying huge wrapped gifts.

Didn't they know about gift cards? Or online shopping? Granted she had a couple of small things in her luggage for Lara's kids, but they barely took up any room.

Ally prided herself on travelling light.

"Two days before Christmas and you didn't expect it to be crowded?" her assistant laughed.

"Well, Christmas Eve and Day are usually quiet; that's why they're usually my favourite days to fly," she said, scowling at a man who'd almost rolled his suitcase right over her toes.

"Because most people spend those days with family, not travelling on vacation," Mel said. "Which reminds me, you're all set for your usual Clearwater Beach hotel. As soon as Christmas is done, you'll be en route to palm trees and sunshine."

Which to Ally right about now, sounded like heaven.

CHAPTER 2

*S*he certainly wouldn't be getting any sunshine and palm trees in upstate Maine.

Looking around again at the crammed airport, Ally started to doubt whether she'd in fact made the right decision visiting Lara and her family for the holidays, rather than going straight to Florida.

But time spent with her old friend was long overdue and since she hadn't yet visited her friend's house, and rarely took time off from her tech consulting business, this time of year was a good opportunity as any.

"Thanks Mel," she said to her assistant now. "Enjoy your time off, and Merry Christmas."

Out of breath a little from running in heels, Ally scrambled to check in at the other airline's digital kiosk with only minutes to spare.

As her boarding pass printed, a sudden horror filled her when she saw the seat number printed next to her name. Not only was this the first time in recent memory she hadn't been upgraded, but to add insult to injury, they had the nerve to ask her to board in the *final* group.

Ally had been pretty much royalty on the biggest airline in the country for the last four years in a row thanks to her weekly travel schedule and copious airmiles.

SkyAir rewarded her for her loyalty by treating her like gold. She was usually the first one on the aircraft, whereupon she almost always enjoyed a complimentary upgrade to first or business class.

What would it be like to fly as a regular person again?

She barely had time to think about what lay ahead as she hurried onwards to her gate.

"Last call, boarding group #5," someone called over the loudspeaker just as she arrived. Looking around the gate, Ally saw only four other people waiting to board.

She quickly scanned her pass and wheeled her bag through, only to find the line at a standstill on the jet bridge.

No doubt the passengers already onboard were searching for overhead space or playing musical chairs with their fellow seat mates trying to secure seats next to the family members they were traveling with.

As if it would be so difficult to spend a two hour flight apart.

"Ma'am," a flight attendant approached her then. "I'm afraid we are going to have to check your luggage today."

"Excuse me?" Ally asked, in the hope she'd misheard. Her bag was TSA approved. It fit perfectly in the overhead storage compartment and was just the right size to hold her clothing, her work computer and toiletries. This lady had to be mistaken.

"Overhead storage is limited on these smaller puddle hoppers," she explained pleasantly. "Don't worry, we'll just store it beneath the hold and it will be waiting for you at the carousel on the other side."

Worry wasn't the right word. Annoyed was more like it. Though not wanting to prolong

the boarding process any further, Ally reluctantly handed over her case, first grabbing her
garment bag off the top.

"OK, well is there somewhere on board I
could hang this maybe?" she asked.

"We only have a small area for the crew's
items. We're not supposed to, but that dress is
gorgeous. It would be a real shame if it got
wrinkled."

"Thank you," Ally smiled gratefully, as the
attendant took the garment bag and headed
back out the gate.

A little bit of separation anxiety kicked in
and she felt compelled to watch as her trusty
suitcase and favourite dress were spirited away
somewhere.

It occurred to Ally then she hadn't arranged
for a bag tag, but before she had time to get the
flight attendant's attention, the line started
moving again and she needed to keep up.

Ally attempted one final peek behind, when
the line once again stopped abruptly and she
collided into a taller man in front. His plaid
sports coat felt soft again her cheek and she
was close enough to see the slight wear in the
leather patches at the elbows.

Assuming he was older based on his style of clothing, when he turned around she was surprised to find that he was in fact, much younger - likely in his early thirties, just like her.

And cute.

"Pardon me," he apologised gently, his blue eyes laser- focused on hers and normally, the intensity of such a gaze would make Ally uncomfortable.

But this gave her time to study his face. She could see that his eyes also had specks of green, his nose was straight and his square jaw line was covered with light stubble. He looked like the kind of guy who would normally be clean shaven, but for some reason had skipped his morning shave for a day or two.

"No, my fault," she mumbled. "I wasn't paying attention."

Ally was almost sorry when he broke their eye contact as the line began to move again, leaving her to stare at the back of his head once more.

Maybe boarding last wasn't so bad after all.

CHAPTER 3

A few more minutes passed before Ally was finally able to board the aircraft and locate her seat.

The sight of the narrow, cramped coach class seat after traveling primarily in the comforts of first class was a rude awakening, and deflated her spirits yet again.

The seat appeared to be only about two feet wide, the armrests were narrow and metal and it clearly didn't have a footrest.

Even at only 5' 3" she still had to crouch down and scoot her legs sideways to fit into it. Though at least she was seated in the aisle and could possibly stretch out her legs a bit that way.

She spent the final minutes before take off on her phone trying to get through all unread work emails that had come in since she'd exited the taxi.

One was from a client confirming a conference call for the 23rd and Ally updated her calendar. She would be in Maine for that one. Lara surely had to have a spare room or some private space she could take the call from, so this shouldn't be a problem.

She made it through another seven or so emails before she heard the dreaded announcement.

"Ladies and gentleman, please switch all cellphones to flight mode, power down computers and other electronics equipment and safely stow them."

Ally harrumphed. How much more pleasant the flying experience would be if someone could figure out a way for passengers to use their phones while in flight?

Not that airlines seemed at all concerned these days with their customer's comfort. The small seat and lack of overhead storage space on this one were alone a testament to that.

Loss of productivity was certainly an

inconvenience, but on the bright side at least she could use this time to unwind and read. About the only time she got the opportunity to indulge in reading just for pleasure. So at least there was that to look forward to.

A couple of minutes after take-off, the drinks cart pulled up along side Ally's seat before she even had a chance to unfasten her seat belt.

She brought her elbow in towards her body to prevent it from inadvertently being bumped with the sharp edges of the metal cart. The arm rest was way too narrow for even her elbow to comfortably rest.

"Can I get you a drink ma'am?"

Ally smiled, thinking how a chilled glass of wine would be just the thing to help her relax for the almost two hour flight. "I'll have a glass of chardonnay if you have it."

"Sure. That will be $8. Cash only."

It has been such a long time since she had flown coach that Ally had completely forgotten that drinks were extra! She reached for her purse, but already knew she didn't have any cash on her. Carrying paper these days was like lugging around a stone and chisel, outdated to say the least.

Was this airline the final frontier of the digital revolution?

"Actually, maybe just some water."

"Sure. That will be $2."

Water was no longer free either?

Frustrated, Ally leaned back into the head-rest of her seat, wishing she had stopped for something before she boarded.

"You know what, I'll pass - I don't have any cash on me right now."

She swallowed, her throat already begin-ning to feel dry at the thought of two hours without anything to drink.

"Here, I've got it."

Ally looked up as she heard a man's voice pipe up from somewhere nearby. Across the aisle, one row behind and diagonal to her own seat was the guy with the plaid sports coat she'd bumped into while boarding.

And much to her embarrassment, he was extending a couple of dollars towards the flight attendant.

"Thank you, that's very kind," she said. "But I'm fine really."

The flight attendant hesitated a little at the guy's outstretched hand, unsure what to do.

"Please - I insist." He nodded and the attendant duly accepted on her behalf.

"Thank you," Ally smiled and took a sip from the plastic cup once it was set on her tray table, while trying to think of how to properly thank the generous stranger.

"Not a problem," he said, as the cart moved on.

"Here, let me pay you back." She tapped her phone screen, and began to pull up her mobile banking app. "If you just tell me your email address, I can Revolut it to you now."

"It's only two dollars, I think I'll survive. In fact, I have more if you really want that wine."

She chuckled. "If we hit any turbulence I may take you up on that." The man reached for his wallet once again, not seeming to pick up on her lighthearted tone. "Hey, I was just joking, honestly."

"Well, the offer is there."

"Thanks." Ally moved her gaze to the back of the seat in front, avoiding more eye contact. The feeling of being indebted to this stranger for his kind act was foreign to her.

It had been a long time since she'd wanted anything that she'd been unable to provide for herself. Even long before her mother died really.

Even during her last relationship, Ally was more often than not the one footing the bill when they went out for dinner.

"I take it you don't fly this airline often?" The helpful stranger spoke again.

"First time."

He offered a knowing smile and Ally found herself unsure of what to do next. For some reason, she didn't want their conversation to end.

"What are you reading?" she asked, noticing the book he had resting on his lap.

When he held it up, she recognised the name of a bestselling author.

"Oh, snap. I've actually just started his series; I'm almost done with the first book. I was hoping to finish it … aw, damn." Just then she remembered her device was in her carry-on bag. The one the flight attendant had whisked away earlier.

When the stranger looked puzzled, she explained this to him.

"I just realised my e-reader is in my luggage. They made me check it."

"They took mine too. The flight's so busy I guess," he shrugged, while Ally wondered what she'd do now to pass the time.

The guy turned back to his book, but then stopped. "I can read aloud if you like. I've been told I have a voice for radio. Or is that a face."

She couldn't help but giggle at his cheesy joke. It reminded her of what Mel referred to as a 'dad joke'.

The kind of joke that would embarrass a teenager if it had been their father making it. Having grown up without a dad, Ally was never able to fully relate to the expression. The thought of a little embarrassment seemed like a small price to pay.

"Henry looks over the horizon in search of …" He read from his book in a dramatic tone, while the passenger seated next to him shot a stern look, clearly not amused.

"Guess he's not a radio fan," Ally leaned across and whispered. "But don't worry - I'll be fine. Enjoy yours in peace. And thanks again for the water."

"No problem." He winked. "But maybe next

time you should rethink your reliance on digital."

Ally smiled. She didn't have the heart to tell him that digital was not only her job, but pretty much her life.

She didn't know what she'd do without tech. As it was, missing her iPad on this flight was like missing an arm.

Instead, she turned back and closed her eyes, suddenly exhausted by her hectic day.

And before Ally knew it, she'd relaxed into a deep and peaceful slumber.

CHAPTER 4

he next thing Ally felt was someone patting her arm. Startled, she sat up in her seat and looked wildly around, trying to remember where she was.

"Must've been a nice dream," the flight attendant who'd just woken her teased, "flight's landed."

Ally scrambled to get up, only to find her neck stiff and her legs heavy. Further adding to her confusion was the fact that she seemed to be the very last person on board.

She looked around, wondering how the passenger sitting next to her in the window seat had made it past without her waking. And then instinctively she glanced at the seat across the aisle where the helpful guy had been sitting, and found herself wishing it weren't empty.

It would have been nice to thank him again before they parted ways.

Then her cheeks felt hot at the thought of him seeing her fast asleep while making his way off the plane. What if her mouth had been wide open with a line of drool down the side of her mouth? What if the altitude made her snore?

She shook her head in an attempt to rid her mind of these embarrassing thoughts.

Hopping up, she automatically opened the overhead bin out of habit to retrieve her case, forgetting that it wasn't in there. It was only when the flight attendant returned with her garment bag that she remembered she would have to wait for it at the carousel.

As she exited through to the terminal, Ally was greeted by the sound of tinny Christmas tunes in the background.

She couldn't understand for the life of her why an airport would play background music so loudly, let alone the old festive favourite that was currently blaring. A shame no one could come up with any new original holiday tunes anymore. Hearing the same songs year after year was a bit depressing.

As she approached the quiet carousel, she realised that at least one advantage to being the last person off the plane was everyone else had already picked up their stuff and she wouldn't need to fight for her spot.

Her case was the only one left on the carousel, and cut a lonely sight, wandering round and round the circuit.

Ally grabbed it by the handle and hoisted it up, noticing that it felt a little heftier than she remembered.

She really was exhausted.

As she set off to exit the terminal, she quickly powered her phone back on to figure out where she was meeting Lara, frowning a little when she realised how little battery it had left.

Her best friend answered after one ring, and she strained to hear over the background music. "Hey, I've just landed, you here?" She heard a baby crying on the other end of the line.

"Almost there sweetie," she cooed, in a tone

Ally had never heard before. "Be right there!" she yelled back into the phone then, sounding much more like the Lara she knew.

Outside the building, almost as soon as the phone disconnected, Ally spied a mini van pull forward to the curb.

One hand was still on the wheel, but as soon as she spotted the messy heap of dark blonde hair pilled on top of the driver's head, she knew it was Lara.

Her friend's hair had been the first thing Ally noticed about her when they first met back in college.

She was sitting behind Lara n an art history class, and while the professor was showing slides of Hagia Sophia, she was memorised by the way her soft curls bounced each time she moved her head.

Ally had always wanted to be able to do her own hair the same way, but hers was poker straight. Her mom had been the only one who was able to get it to cooperate in any way.

One day during class, she finally decided to ask the girl how she did it. Lara was only too happy to show her, and they were pretty much inseparable the rest of college.

Ally always felt such a sense of nostalgia and joy when she remembered her carefree years as college student.

She had initially selected History as her major, since it was something she was endlessly interested in. Luckily enough, by the time she was a sophomore, her college advisor was kind enough to show her the starting salaries of various majors.

Ally's mother's declining health meant she would be on her own soon enough and she immediately switched to Computer Science, the top-paying field at the time.

Now, one hand on her luggage, the other raised in greeting, she walked towards the mini van that was stopped in the designated pick-up area.

"Riley, pick that up for your sister and she'll stop crying," she heard as she approached the van. Even with the windows rolled up, her best friend's voice was still audible.

She waited a few seconds before tapping lightly on the widow with her knuckles, hoping the noise didn't startle everyone.

"Thank you honey," Ally heard, before Lara turned around and looked out her window.

She beamed and hurriedly undid her seat belt as she reached for the door handle. "Hey big city girl!" her friend exclaimed jumping from the car and throwing her arms around her. "Let me help you with your bags."

"No, don't worry, I've just got one. Pop the trunk and I'll throw it in."

Ally went to the rear of the car, peeking inside the widows at her adorable five year old godson and brand new goddaughter.

This would be her first time meeting Charlotte since she was born six months earlier. Another reason for this visit since she would get to do so while she was still a baby. Something her schedule hadn't allowed five years ago when Riley was born.

When Lara and her husband eventually did make a trip with Riley to Boston he was already walking by the time Ally got to meet him.

Opening the trunk, Ally hesitated when she saw the mountain of toys, fresh diapers and what appeared to be trash, piled almost as high as the back of the seat.

"Just throw it anywhere, don't worry - nothing back there is important," Lara called back and Ally followed her friend's instructions and hoisted the suitcase up and onto the shortest pile of the debris, once again laying her dress neatly over the top of it.

"Aunt Ally!" Riley squealed once she'd settled in to the passenger seat. It took her a few minutes to situate her feet since the floor was also littered with food wrappers.

"There you are honey. Riley you are even more handsome than the last time I saw you."

"Can I play some games on your phone?"

Lara swiped her outstretched hand past her neck, the universal gesture for 'do that and I'll kill you.'

"Sorry bud, my phone's almost dead. I need to charge it." That was actually the truth though. Ally glanced down at screen and saw she was now at 10%. Bummer.

Another downside of the different airline - there were usually charging stations in the armrests of her usual. But this one had been basic and without frills - to say the least.

"We are having a tech free Christmas," Lara supplied.

"Sounds like fun," Ally said, with as much sarcasm as possible.

"We want to spend the holidays connecting as a family without all these distractions. And it's not good for developing young brains to be so overly stimulated."

"Poor kids. My mom certainly never limited mine, and look how I turned out."

"Exactly, a cautionary tale."

Ally laughed and moved aside empty juice boxes on the car's console in an attempt to locate a phone charger.

"Lara you have got to be kidding me..." she said, holding up the end of the adapter.

"What?"

"Your phone must be at least two years old if you still use this to charge it."

"Like I have time to keep track of how old my phone is. It still works, so why would I buy a new one?"

Ally shook her head in amazement, realising she'd need to wait until she could unpack her own.

"Oh I can't believe you're finally here!" her friend enthused. "Especially on Christmas. I thought for sure you'd have made plans with Gary. How is that going?"

Ally made a face. "It's not - going I mean.

According to him we were never actually dating in the first place. Really fooled me."

"Unbelieveable. Men these days."

"So what are the plans for tonight?" she asked, changing the subject. "We heading out somewhere? I checked the OpenTable app but couldn't find anything ... "

"Like for dinner?" Lara bit her lip. "With these two, restaurants are more trouble than they're worth these days."

"I can imagine. What time do they go to bed? We could head out then."

"Ha! By the time I get them both down I'm almost ready to pass out myself."

"Oh, sorry." Ally did her best to hide her disappointment. She had been looking forward to a night out with her best friend forever. Although she supposed it was foolish to think they'd be able to recreate the kind of fun they used to have in college.

"Don't be sorry, I'm sure not. I used to think bar hopping was so fun. Now it just seems empty compared to what I have now."

Lara looked into her rearview mirror at her smiling baby and fidgeting toddler in the backseat. "I've some pizza back at the house. We'll show you what real fun is."

"Great, I like pizza." As Ally looked over at her friend in her oversized sweatshirt, a Christmas elf on the front and her fuzzy black sweatpants, it was hard to remember what Lara was like before she become a mother.

How was this the same woman who used to complain at 2am when the bars would close because she didn't want to go home?

"Anyway, better to save our energies for the Snow Ball," Lara added then. "I've hired a sitter so we can go all out, hair, false eyelashes, the works. So I really hope you packed a knockout dress."

"Sure did."

"Oh we're going to have so much fun! Tomorrow is the ice maze, and then the tree lighting. You'll really like that one."

Ally swallowed hard. A bunch of people standing around in the freezing cold waiting for someone to flip the switch on a few lights didn't exactly sound like a rip-roaring time.

And the ice maze sounded very much like a kids thing.

Oh well, she'd get into the spirit of all this stuff, for Lara's sake at least.

It was a couple of days, tops. After that Ally would be chilling beneath the palm trees, pina colada in hand, Christmas a distant memory.

Heaven.

CHAPTER 5

*A*fter a forty-five minute drive through mostly woodlands, Lara turned onto a dimly lit road.

"Country living at it's finest," her friend declared.

Out of the darkness, a massive house appeared and Ally made no attempt to hide her surprise.

"Uh you didn't think to tell me you lived in a mansion?"

She was shocked enough when six years ago Lara broke the news that she was leaving Boston with her new husband Mark. The two women had done everything together, it was hard for Ally to imagine them living in different states.

Mark's grandmother had just passed and left them a house in his home town. He was also apparently the family heir to a small business, a restaurant and a few other things in the place.

Funny how Lara, the one who'd stuck with Art as her major in college, knowing she'd likely never make a lot of money and didn't care, ended up living in a house like this.

Wealth and material things never mattered to her best friend though, which is probably why Lara never told her about this place.

All these years, Ally had felt sorry for her friend living in Hicksville. But now, she felt a bit sorry for herself thinking how her entire apartment could probably fit into her friend's foyer!

Lara proceeded to pull into the wraparound driveway with trees surrounding either side, all lit by beautiful white fairy lights. A coating of fresh white snow sat on top of each tree as if it had been hand-placed by a professional decorator.

Columns surrounding the porch were

decorated with alternating red and green festive garland.

It all looked like something out of a Christmas card.

"Nice isn't it? It belonged to Mark's grandmother. Way too much space for us, but it means a lot to him raising his family here."

"I'll say. It's like the McAllister's place in *Home Alone*."

Ally grabbed her bag and helped Riley out of his car seat while Lara picked up the baby carrier and headed inside.

A massive Christmas tree took up over half the entryway, and every branch had beautiful, distinctive ornaments dangling. The angel on top was pretty much level with a grand second-story staircase.

The whole effect was magnificent, truly like something out of a movie and Ally almost thought of asking Lara for a map of the place, just in case she got lost.

"Mommy, I'm hungry," Riley declared, as he threw off his coat.

"Alright, let's get the pizza in. Will you show Aunt Ally where the guest room is? I'm sure she's dying to get out of those work clothes."

Ally glanced down at her dress and pumps. She had never really thought of her outfit as 'work clothes' before. But perhaps something casual would indeed be more appropriate for pizza and playing with the kids.

She headed upstairs, struggling a little as she hefted her case up the grand, seemingly never-ending stair case.

Inside the guest room, she threw it onto the bed and undid the zipper. Then throwing the lid back, she stopped and frowned.

A beige sweater lay on top, a fancy expensive looking cashmere one that Ally couldn't recall packing.

Or *owning* for that matter.

Moving it aside, her frown deepened with what she found underneath; a bunch of books and notebooks.

Three had the same cover, with mountains in the background - proper books. Ally didn't even own four hardcopy books, much less three of the same.

She continued to dig, hoping that whomever put these relics in her suitcase on top of her stuff, wasn't also a thief that would have taken her phone charger.

But came up empty handed, as she pushed aside a tuxedo, a pair of slippers, until finally realization dawned.

This was *not* her bag!

Yes, it was the same type and model as the one she'd taken on every trip since she founded her tech consultant business six years ago, but it definitely wasn't the one she'd boarded the plane with.

She must have grabbed it by mistake. But no, this was the only one left on the carousel, which was why she'd taken it in the first place.

Which meant that someone else had picked up hers.

They were the one who had made the mistake.

What on earth was she going to do?

CHAPTER 6

*A*lly fell backwards onto the bed as the realisation sunk in even further.

She had no laptop, no VPN, no phone charger. Let alone personal belongings, like a toothbrush or makeup or underwear even!

How was this possible? And what should she do? Once the phone on her battery died, she'd be completely cut off from the outside world.

Ally struggled to keep her breathing even, as she went to find her friend.

"Lara!" she called helplessly down the hallway. "All of my stuff is gone."

Her friend came out of the master bedroom

with baby Charlotte on her hip. "What do you mean - gone?"

"I grabbed the wrong bag at the airport. Well, I mean I didn't - someone else did and I got this one instead which obviously isn't mine, so I don't have any stuff and ..."

"OK calm down. I can lend you anything you need for the moment - I've got spare toiletries and we can grab the basics in town ..."

"No, my stuff, work stuff. My laptop was in here and my charger and iPad ... I have important calls and a couple of Zoom meetings coming up - I can't miss them."

"You'll get it all back in no time, I'm sure. Just relax. First things first, let's get you some clothes and then we can call the airline. With your status they'll probably hire a limo to hand-deliver it all back to you."

If only it had happened on my airline, Ally thought, unable to share her friend's optimism. Taking a deep breath, she followed Lara into her bedroom, doing her best to focus on the clothing options she was offering, but all she could think about was a finding a way to get her bag back.

"I know - I'll get my assistant on it. She'll be able to figure it out with the airline."

"Great idea."

Though Ally wasn't sure exactly how, since the bag she had didn't have an airline identification tag. And neither did hers. Which meant like hers, it must also have been stowed unexpectedly.

Then she groaned, remembering that Mel had officially logged off for the holidays.

Still, she was sure she wouldn't mind, and pinged her a quick text, before her phone ran out and she was *seriously* stuck.

"If you could just lend me something to wear tonight to sleep in? And maybe something for tomorrow morning at that ice maze thing just in case."

With the arm that wasn't holding her baby, Lara reached for a pair of pants draped over the arm of a rocking chair. "These are thermals. You can wear them under these jeans tomorrow. And I'll find you a sweater and some boots."

"Thanks." Ally examined the pants trying to determine if they'd fit her.

"And for tonight, take this." Lara threw her

two large flannel items, a pair of decidedly unfeminine pyjamas, the kind a grandfather might wear.

Ally returned to the guest room to try on the nightclothes her friend had been kind enough to lend her. It felt strange to be wearing pyjamas when she hadn't yet eaten dinner, but the feeling of the warm flannel against her skin was too good to pass up.

She caught a glimpse of herself in the floor length mirror on the back of the door before heading down the stairs.

Despite her worries, the festive red and green and poinsettia flowered pattern made her smile at her own reflection.

Never in a million years could Ally have imagined herself wearing Christmas pjs, but something about it had almost magically made her feel better already.

CHAPTER 7

"Merry Christmas," Jake Turner called to the driver as he exited the cab in front of the chateau his family rented every year in this Maine small town for the holidays.

As a kid, having to spend Christmas so far from his friends in Boston was a total drag, but as an adult, he anticipated this break from hectic city life.

"Jakey!" his younger sister Meghan squealed and ran towards him from the doorway. She had her arms wrapped around him before he could even set his luggage down.

"Hello to you too. Did I miss anything good?"

He hated the fact that he wasn't able to join the rest of the family when they'd arrived a couple of days ago. But the holiday shopping season was a busy time for his profession.

His publisher had somehow landed a book signing at Barnes & Noble and being in desperate need of exposure (and sales), Jake was only too happy to agree.

"Just the same ole, same ole," said Meghan. "I'd much rather hear about your book signing."

He let out a big sigh.

"That bad?"

"Just wasn't quite the turnout we'd hoped."

"I'm sorry. But hey, don't worry about it. Your job is to write, theirs is to take care of sales. Your new book is amazing. If that publisher can't sell it, maybe you should just find someone else."

Even in adulthood his baby sister thought he could do no wrong.

"The business is changing now, though. According to my agent, I need to connect more with my readers. She keeps trying to get me on social media." He wrinkled his nose.

"Well, I actually agree with her on that one.

You are *way* behind the times. A real techno dinosaur."

"Not behind, I just prefer my privacy. I know that kind of makes me an anomaly in our generation," he laughed.

"Hey, enough about work, hurry up and get changed out of that old man history professor vibe you've got going on," Melanie urged, her nose wrinkling at the sight of his jacket. "Everyone's here and we're just about to eat."

"Great, I'm starving. Let me just drop my stuff up and get settled in."

The chateau was rustic in the most literal sense of the word, and all of the ceilings were made of exposed dark wooden beams. Though the open fire and twinkling lights of the Christmas tree in the living area made it wonderfully welcoming and festive, especially for family gatherings.

Jake took off upstairs to his usual room, the same one he stayed in every year.

Putting his suitcase on the bench along the end of the bed, he hurried to unzip it and retrieve his slippers for starters, so he could get out of these constricting leather shoes.

But upon opening the case, Jake knew

immediately that something wasn't right. He most certainly didn't pack a pair of sparkly, four inch heels. Nor a pearl-studded clutch. Or an entire department stores-worth of colourful bikinis…

What the…?

'You've got to be kidding me…"

He'd picked up the wrong bag at the airport. At the realisation, a panic ignited with such force that his heart began to beat rapidly.

Jake tried to calm himself so he could think. He quickly zipped the bag back up, almost as if he was doing something illegal, and raced back downstairs, signalling his sister out to the hallway.

"My bag - I grabbed the wrong bag at the airport," he whispered loudly to Meghan, trying her utmost to stay out of earshot of any others.

She gave him a curious look. "OK, I'm sure we can call the airline. They probably still have yours. Calm down."

"I can't calm down! Is Heidi in there?" Jake indicated the living room as he paced back and forth, his mind racing.

"No, she's in town with Mom - why? Oh,

no!" Meghan suddenly realised the seriousness of the situation. "You don't mean to tell me *that* was in the…"

"It was." Jake looked around wildly. "Which is why I have to get that bag back. Now."

CHAPTER 8

a little later Ally was greeted by the most wonderful cooking smell as she entered Lara's kitchen downstairs.

Her friend stood by the quartz island in the middle of her massive gourmet kitchen, looking all the world like a culinary professional.

Besides the jaunty elf hat she was sporting, and Ally had to giggle at the sight.

Lara pulled a steaming hot flatbread pizza from the oven and set it in the middle of an impressive spread of delicious-looking salads and dips. She then drizzled olive oil out of a very fancy green bottle over the mushroom and goat cheese pizza toppings.

"Hope you're hungry…" she sang as Ally got closer.

"Starving. Though I wish you hadn't gone to so much trouble. When you said pizza in the car, I just assumed…"

"That I'd be serving you junk? Like I would do such a thing." Lara grabbed half a lemon and squeezed it over a large bowl of baby arugula, topped with freshly shaved parmesan.

"Boys dinner!"she yelled and as if on cue, her husband Mark and little Riley came racing into the kitchen and each grabbed a plate from the pile on the counter.

"Riley eats arugula? And mushrooms?" Ally asked in surprise.

"Oh yes, he's very adventurous. Grab a plate and dig in."

She tried to remember the last time she'd eaten a meal that someone else had prepared for her, and sadly couldn't.

Once everyone had a full plate, they all gathered around the kitchen table to eat together. The lights were low and soft festive tunes played in the background.

It was unbelievable warm and cosy and Ally

got a sense of why her friend loved her little family so much.

This was ... wonderful.

"Aunt Ally, want to see my trains?" Riley asked when they'd finished eating.

"Sure, I'd love to."

He grabbed her by the hand and almost yanked her out of her seat in his excitement, leading her to the corner of the living area where there were almost 50 pieces of wooden train tracks on the floor, and dozens magnetic trains.

The warm glow of the fireplace lit up the family room and made it magical. Five stockings hung from the mantel, each awaiting a visit from Santa. Ally could only imagine the excitement the kids would experience on Christmas morning.

Riley sat on the floor and immediately went to work connecting the pieces of the tracks. His eyebrows furrowed as he concentrated on his design.

"Ally would you like some more wine?" Lara, ever the gracious hostess, called out from the kitchen.

"Sure - if you are."

"Ha! If I drink this late at night I'll be asleep before anyone else. But don't let that stop you."

"No no, I'm busy over here. But thank you."

In no time, Riley had built a massive circular train track, complete with a bridge and two junctures. He slid his six engine train around the corners, making whistling sounds.

Ally stood a few feet in front straddling the tracks with one leg on each side. "Tunnel!" she teased playfully, causing Riley to look up with a huge smile.

He expertly steered his cars past, ducking to fit under and screamed in delight as he passed.

"Again!" he shouted, still laughing.

This time, Ally got down with her hands and knees on either side of the tracks and just as he cleared her tunnel, she grabbed him from behind in a giant bear hug. "You forgot to pay the toll."

He erupted with laughter as she lifted him into the air and Charlotte began to giggle too, in the way only a small baby can.

She continued to play with Riley, coming up with at least twenty different tunnel challenges, until Mark announced it was time for bed.

"But Dad …" he whined, not happy the fun was over and Ally had to stop herself from objecting also, not wanting their game to end. She was enjoying herself a lot more than she'd expected.

"Will you be here tomorrow?" Riley asked before heading upstairs.

"I sure will, and we're going to have so much fun. Tomorrow is the ice maze, right?"

"Yay!"

After, Ally insisted on cleaning up so Lara could rock Charlotte. She couldn't help but stare at the baby's sweet face as she nestled close to her mother and closed her eyes.

Lara caressed her baby's head, and Ally wondered if her wispy blonde hair felt as soft as it looked.

"I'm so glad you decided to come and spend Christmas with us," her friend said in a soft whisper.

Ally nodded, almost afraid to answer.

"It's OK, she is a very sound sleeper. Has to be, with a five year old brother."

"I know. And I can't believe this is only our second Christmas together. Remember that year, the big snow storm when I was marooned at your place?"

They'd dressed up in two of the ugliest holiday sweaters and thrown together some food from whatever was in Lara's fridge, then spent the rest of the evening talking until the early hours.

The next morning, Ally awoke to a present under the small tabletop tree in her friend's place. The tag read 'from Santa'.

She still had the fuzzy socks that were inside the perfectly wrapped package.

Her friend had always been Christmas crazy but it was only now that Ally was beginning to appreciate it.

"I promise, *this* will be a Christmas to remember," Lara said. "This town goes all out with the holiday cheer and decorations - and the ice maze. Plus the big Christmas Eve Snow Ball. Honestly, by the time I'm finished with you, you won't have time to think, much less work."

At the mention of work, Ally felt her heart deflate afresh at the realisation she was without any of her conferencing equipment.

And her phone battery was now running perilously low.

"Do you have an office I could maybe use for my meetings tomorrow?" she asked Lara.

"Yeah, we have a den, next room over. Very quiet and private. But why do you have meetings set up anyway? Who wants to work on the holidays?"

But Ally had already gone to check out the den, making a mental checklist of what she would need; phone, computer, an extra monitor, decent internet.

She sat in the large leather desk chair, powering up the desktop and ran a quick diagnostic test to determine Lara's wifi speed. Much to her surprise, it wasn't fast enough to run her mobile conferencing software, even if she did have it. It wasn't even fast enough to stream a movie.

How on earth did Lara and Mark survive?

Going back to the family room, she made a mental note to see about getting their internet speed upgraded.

It would be her gift to them for being such gracious hosts.

Ally was tempted to take out her phone and

create a reminder for herself, but until she secured a charger, she had to maintain what little battery life was left.

The thought of being completely without her phone too was enough to make her panic. It was her lifeline; she'd be completely lost without it.

There was still no reply from Mel about her missing luggage, and she hoped against hope that her assistant hadn't well and truly logged off for the Christmas break.

But why wouldn't she? The last time they'd spoken, as far as Mel was concerned, Ally was all set.

Just as she was about to express these worries to Lara, she noticed her friend's eyes were closed while Charlotte curled up against her chest.

Ally stopped, in awe of the cosy maternal scene.

Then Lara's eyes flickered open. "Oops, sorry about that. she's been teething, so I'm a little behind on my sleep."

"Sounds rough. You should get to bed."

"I feel terrible though. Here you are on your first night and I'm falling asleep on you." Lara stood up, gingerly carrying a still dozing Charlotte. "Look, try to get some sleep yourself and try not to worry about the luggage thing. It'll be returned in no time. In fact, I'm sure whoever took yours is already figuring out a way to get it back."

"Hope so." Ally nodded and quietly followed upstairs in her friend's wake.

Still fuelled by the trauma of losing her suitcase and the nap she took earlier on the airplane, she wasn't ready for sleep though.

She ran through any potential options for entertainment in her mind. No iPad, laptop, just an almost-dead phone - and no TV in the guest room either.

It wasn't looking very promising.

Wandering around the bed, her gaze drifted to the suitcase and the books she had discovered earlier.

She picked up a hardback and rang a finger across the embossed author name on the front: J.T. Walker.

Never heard of him.

She flipped the book to its back cover, whereupon reviewers sang their praises for this apparent fictional masterpiece.

Huh.

Ally moved the suitcase onto the floor and crawled into bed with the book.

Perhaps a few chapters of this would be just what she needed to drift off.

CHAPTER 9

*A*lly awoke the following morning to the sound of footsteps. Having lived alone the last fifteen years, it was enough to rouse her from a deep sleep.

Her body begged her to close her eyes again, but the realisation of what had happened the day before awakened her quick-smart.

She had a mission to accomplish.

"Morning!" Lara greeted her over a mug of coffee.

"Please tell me you have lots more of that," Ally groaned, walking into the kitchen mid-yawn.

"A whole pot. Help yourself."

She duly grabbed a mug from the cupboard

that Lara gestured towards, and filled it to the brim.

"I hope Charlotte didn't wake you last night."

"Not at all, I was just late up reading. I got stuck into a really great book."

Lara's stared at her, surprised.

Ally shrugged. "I found it in that other person's suitcase. And as crazy as it sounds, I think the owner of the suitcase might be the writer of the book."

Lara frowned. "I don't follow. Why would you think that?" she asked, while whisking pancake batter.

"It had three copies of the same book in it, plus a notebook with handwritten outlines of what I think is going to be a sequel. And he's got some nice clothes. Rich guy's clothes."

"You looked through a stranger's stuff? What else did you do, try on his clothes?"

"No, I wasn't trying to be nosy. I just thought maybe there'd be a name or a phone number in there, some way of contacting the guy."

"Good idea. Was there?"

"No. Though he must travel quite a bit, he

had all of his toiletries in travel size and they had been used before." It took Ally ages to realise what a time saver it was to have a special set of travel toiletries always ready to go.

"You're like a detective. What else did you find?"

"A few really nice cashmere sweaters, a pair of slippers, some socks and a carefully folded tux even. The quality of everything was top notch too."

Lara made a face. "Sounds like what my grandpa packs when he travels."

"But if I'm right, and he is the author of the books, then I also know his name - well kinda. J.T. Walker."

"Great, well that's a good start isn't it?"

"You'd think. I googled him to see if there was maybe a social media profile, or author website I could reach him at, but there were little to no personal details at all online, just book stockists and reviews. If his clothes are that nice he must be pretty successful. So strange."

Ally wrapped her hands around her warm coffee cup and savoured a few sips, waiting for the caffeine to activate the rest of her brain so she could think of a way to contact JT Walker.

Bad wifi or not though, she'd need to use Lara's desktop computer, because thanks to that little spate of online research in the early hours to find out more about the author, her phone battery had finally given up the ghost.

Though at least she'd be able to secure a charger today. While Ally was confident her assistant would surely come up with the goods in the meantime, she was feeling a lot brighter about the prospect of getting her bag back.

Of all the things she did on a daily basis as a tech consultant, locating this J.T. Walker guy should be a piece of cake.

CHAPTER 10

*J*ake opened his eyes and was relieved to see the sun was finally up.

That meant he no longer had to force himself to try and sleep like he'd been doing for the last eight hours, while his mind continued to bombard him with different ways of potentially getting his bag back.

Usually, when he found himself unable to sleep, he'd use the time to write, so not having his notebook was adding injury to insult. Especially when he had a plot to outline - preferably by the end of holidays.

He'd make a stop at the general store in

town for a new one though; one thing at least, that was easy to replace.

The evening before he and Meghan had racked their brains till the early hours to see if there was anything they could do to locate his bag, but to no avail.

He'd been waiting on the line for almost an hour to speak to somebody from the airline, and in the end they'd told him to lodge a lost property query and they'd get back to him.

The representative seemed bored and patently uninterested in his plight, but Jake thought, she had no real idea what was at stake here.

And it wasn't as though he could tell her either - just in case it made things worse.

Though at least there had been one spark of hope.

"Maybe the person who owns the case you took by mistake, picked up yours?" Meghan had suggested much later, after a family dinner during which Jake spent much of the time fretting. "Did you check it out - see if there's maybe any contact details in there?"

"Good idea."

Telling the others he needed an early night

after the day's travel, Jake was finally able to examine the bag properly.

And mercifully, attached to the top handle, he spied that there was indeed one of those plastic inserts with a business card and - thank goodness - office phone number inside.

But having little choice but to call it a day given the late hour, he planned to call the number first thing, and with luck he'd have his bag (and it's precious contents) back in no time.

Maybe the other person hadn't even realised the mix-up yet?

But when earlier that morning he'd phoned the number for Walters Technology, the line rang out. Not especially surprising given it was so close to Christmas, but what was he going to do now?

"Morning," he greeted Meghan dully, as he entered the kitchen, looking for coffee.

He was relieved she was the only one awake at this early hour. Unlike last night, when he'd no choice but to share the news about the business card in a hush, now they could strategise freely without being overheard.

"You look well rested," she teased, raising an eyebrow.

"Yeah, a bit too much on my mind to sleep."

"Don't worry. I have a lead."

Jake almost dropped his cup.

"You do?"

"Yes, if you weren't so behind the times you could have done this yourself last night. A quick google and I found Walters Tech on social media. It took like, thirty seconds."

Meghan pulled up the page and handed her phone to her brother. From what he could make out it was a generic business page - something to do with electronics and technology, which was already pretty apparent from the company name.

"OK, this is great and all, but how is this going to help? I just tried the number, and there's no reply - presumably they're finished for the holidays."

"Yes, but the business seems like just a smaller one-man show than some big enterprise. According to this, the owner's name is Ally Walters - and *this* is Ally's personal profile," Meghan pointed out with a flourish. "She must've been travelling on the same flight, and if you have her bag, then most likely she has yours." She shrugged. "So now we just need to a way to find Ally. Makes sense actually, that a tech consultant would be carrying that weird-looking charger."

Unfamiliar electronics aside, Jake did his best to be patient, still not understanding how a social media page was going to help him get his bag back - today.

Unless they could send this ... Ally a message somehow?

Though Meghan seemed to have it all figured out. "Now, look at this," she told him, trying to remain patient with him. "See that, at the top of her page?"

Jake looked again at the screen and read a post from someone called Lara Clark which read; *Excited to be setting my high-achieving bestie a real challenge today! Knowing Ally she'll be out by midday.*

He frowned at his sister. "I still don't get it."

"Ally - the woman whose bag you have - is tagged in that post, linking to the ice maze."

He looked blank.

Meghan rolled her eyes. This person, Lara Clark tagged her 'bestie' Ally Walters, who it seems happens to be headed to the ice maze - right here in this town - *today.*

Jake eyes widened. "Oh wow! Good detective work."

That was surprisingly easy actually. He'd go to the ice maze this morning, find this Ally, who by now surely must have also realised the mistake, and would be only too happy to make the switch.

Out by midday...

Finally Jake's heart lifted. He'd have everything back before he knew it.

CHAPTER 11

*A*fter breakfast, Ally spent most of the morning on Lara's phone to the airline, being directed from pillar to post.

But none of the four representatives she spoke with, nor indeed anyone at the airport, could shine a light on the location of her bag.

Nothing had been handed in at the terminal, and with no trackable luggage tag for the airline to trace, by the end of multiple conversations and hours on hold, she was still no closer to being reunited with her bag.

She'd also tried in vain to contact Mel, but her assistant clearly wasn't picking up email or her phone since logging off for the holidays - and certainly not from an unfamiliar landline.

While Lara was adamant Ally could borrow whatever she needed for the duration of the stay, there was still the pressing matter of the upcoming work calls, and indeed the subsequent Florida trip.

She needed to get her stuff back pronto and if it meant chasing down this J.T. person to see if he'd been to one to accidentally take her bag, so be it.

By now she was willing to try *anything*.

But first and foremost, she needed to get her phone back up and running so that she wasn't completely cut off and dependent on Lara for everything.

It was a weird feeling for Ally, being so helpless and out of control like this. But the return of her beloved phone would soon set her back on track.

Now, as she entered the town's general store, she was taken aback at the wide array of items the tiny retailer carried. Everything from hardware items, gifts, home decor, plus books and magazines. Impressive though probably necessary, given it was one of only three stores in the little town.

If you needed something, your choices were

here, the grocery store, or the clothing boutique Ally hoped stocked bikinis in winter. Just in case.

But there was one category of items she wasn't seeing in this place yet, and that was electronics.

"Can I help you ma'am?" an older man greeted from behind the counter and Ally knew from Lara's description that he was the owner of the shop. A true town fixture.

"Yes, I'm in desperate need of a phone charger. Do you have one for this particular model?" she asked, showing him her device.

"Well, I haven't come across that one before, but I have a few that might work, I think." The man proceeded to pull out a large box from under the counter.

It contained six different types of chargers, sadly none of which would work, Ally realised, her spirits dropping. Hers was a brand new model and had only been on the market for a couple of weeks. Clearly the price of early adoption was steep.

She thanked the man for his time, and was just about to leave when she noticed some distinctive looking spiral-bound notebooks near the counter. They reminded her of the one in the suitcase and immediately, she thought of something.

"Hey did anyone come in to buy one of these today by any chance?" she asked, figuring it was a long shot, but what the hell...

He stopped to think. "Come to think of it, yes a little while ago actually. A couple - on their way to the ice maze apparently. He needed gloves too."

Now *this* news was music to Ally's ears. Maybe small town living wasn't as bad as she thought. And she congratulated herself on her good ole fashioned detective skills.

"Did you catch a name by any chance?"

"No didn't get that much - like I said, they were in a hurry. Definitely from out of town though, much like yourself I'd wager."

That made sense too. "Yes, I'm here to visit my friend - she recommended I come here, Lara Clark?"

The man beamed. "Of course I know Lara, and Mark too. Great couple, pillars of this community."

Ally smiled. "They are a great couple. Well, she's actually waiting for me in the car, and we're on our way to the ice maze too, so I'd better get going, but thank you so much for your help."

"No problem. Tell Lara I said hi. And little Riley too."

"I will. But I might need to pop back before tomorrow - besides a charger, I'm also in need of some Christmas gifts for Lara and her family." She sighed, reminding herself again of her current predicament. "You see, I lost my luggage en route here, and if I don't get it back soon I'm out of luck until after Christmas. My gifts, along with my clothes were in there too. About all I have left is a sparkly dress and that's not much use in this weather."

The man smiled. "Coming along to the Snow Ball then? It's a great evening, the holiday highlight of the year in this town."

Ally gulped, not having anticipated the event as that big of a deal. With luck by then she'd be reunited with her shoes too. Otherwise she was going to cut a very sorry sight tomorrow night in her sparkly dress with no accessories, or even decent underwear.

"Well, maybe I'll see you there," the shop owner continued smiling, and Ally nodded politely.

Then, before turning again to leave she thought of something. "That couple … who bought the notebooks earlier - can you tell me what either of them looked like?"

The man thought for a bit. "Well, she was maybe early thirties with long, curly hair, green jacket and grey bobble hat and very friendly like you. He was tall - lighter hair maybe? Wearing corduroy trousers. And a red knit sweater. Typical out of towner stuff." He chuckled.

"Wonderful, thank you so much." Ally headed back to the car to tell Lara what she had learned.

"Guess who could also be on the way to the ice maze?" she said, answering her own question before she even gave her friend a chance to guess. "J.T. must be in town too."

"Well, I hate to sound negative, but we do get a lot of out of towners coming to the ice maze at this time of year. Could be a needle in a haystack."

"I do know whoever bought the notebook is

wearing corduroy pants, and a red sweater," Ally said, proudly filling her in on the couple's description.

Lara wrinkled her nose. "Old guy clothes. Well, at least *that* should narrow it down."

CHAPTER 12

"OK, if this is Lara, how do I find Ally at the ice maze? Or even know what she looks like?" Jake was asking, as he continued to scroll on his sister's phone.

Meghan showed him where to click for Walters Technology, and they both looked for a photo or more pertinent info about Ally, as he scrolled through various pictures of office space, computer equipment, and a few business articles.

They continued to search, hoping to find at least one picture of their mystery woman.

And while her friend had lots of personal photographs on her social media profile, there seemed none at all of Ally.

"This is obviously more of a business page," Meghan pointed out. "All her posts seem to be tagged reviews from clients. And very satisfied ones at that."

Jake began reading some of the rave reviews. Clearly this Ally was very good at what she did. Not that he understood any of the technological lingo.

All these years he had been reluctant to get involved in social media. The idea of posting pictures of his private life for all to see was enough to make his skin crawl.

But if he could make a page like this one, just about his work and perhaps interact with people at arm's length? That might not be so bad.

"Can we send her a message or anything?" he asked Meghan then. "Ask her to meet with us at the maze and maybe bring the bag?"

"We'd have to find out if she has it first. I'll send a friend request and add a little message."

'You're a genius." Jake grinned as she typed away.

He knew he should probably try to relax and just wait to see if this Ally would reply, but again it was so close to Christmas - would she even be checking business messages?

No, the idea of sitting around and not doing anything was impossible - especially considering what was at stake.

He needed to explore all options, including the ice maze.

"I'm going to head down there anyway, see if I can maybe even spot the friend there. She said out by midday right? "

"Ice Maze? Sounds like fun," another voice approaching the kitchen piped up and Jake froze, knowing who it was, but almost afraid to look and confirm his fears.

"Morning Heidi," Meghan greeted in a high voice, as an attractive blonde approached and kissed Jake on the cheek.

"What time were you thinking of heading out?" Heidi asked.

"In about like fifteen minutes or so actually, before it gets too crowded," Jake replied, in the hopes she wouldn't want to tag along. Then he'd have a lot of explaining to do.

"OK, I'll go jump in the shower first."

Before Jake could think of another excuse, his sister beat him to it.

"But I thought Mom needed you for food shopping today. You know, to help with Christmas dinner"

Jake did his best to act calm, as Heidi frowned considering. Then much to his luck, she smiled. "I'd forgotten all about that. You're right, maybe I'll just catch up with you guys later."

And as he and Meghan grabbed their coats and hurried outside to the car, Jake let out the breath he didn't realise he'd been holding.

CHAPTER 13

*A*lly spent the entire car ride to the ice maze thinking of the best way to try and identify the guy who'd bought the notebook, assuming it was the same guy whose case she had.

If he did indeed happen to be J.T. Turner, it was a real shame that there was no author photo on those books.

A needle in a haystack for sure.

Still, as soon as Lara's minivan pulled into the parking lot, she began scanning every person they passed, looking for guy in a red sweater and corduroy trousers and a dark haired woman in a green coat.

"Ally?" Lara's mournful voice pulled her back to the present, as her friend lifted the baby out of her car seat.

"What's up?"

"I can't believe this, but Charlotte's just had an accident - a messy one, by the looks of it. I think I'm going to have to either take her home or to a restroom somewhere to change her."

Ally looked at the baby, still smiling despite the fact that she was indeed a mess, and then back at the very long line already formed at the ice maze entrance.

"Maybe we should all go - looks pretty busy here."

But the look of disappointment in Riley's eyes nearly broke her heart.

"You go on ahead, and maybe just meet us after?" Ally suggested then, grabbing Riley's hand. She was sure they'd be in and out of here in no time.

And anyway she wanted to keep an eye out for red sweater and corduroy pants guy - just in case.

"You sure you don't mind? We'll be back soon."

"Course not. They take virtual pay right?"

Lara chuckled. "This isn't DisneyWorld." She rummaged in her purse and gave Ally a couple of twenties before heading back to the car with Charlotte.

But her friend was only a few feet away when she turned back. "Look!" she urged.

Ally looked to the man her friend was pointing towards, heading their way, and immediately scrunched up her nose. He was indeed wearing the right colour combo, but he looked to be about eighty years old.

Still …

"Excuse me, are you J.T Turner?" Ally asked, when the guy neared the back of the line, feeling a bit ridiculous.

He was far too old to be the owner of the suitcase. And his pants were more olive, not green.

"What did you say?" He leaned closer, obviously a little hard of hearing.

"I'm looking for a man named J.T? Maybe an author?" she repeated, a little louder.

The man smiled, and Ally felt her heart lift a little until he spoke again. "I wish I could help you. The only J.T. I know is long gone. But if you're ever in need of a Malcom, that I could help you with," he added, with a wink.

"Thanks anyway." She grabbed Riley's hand and shuffled back up her place in the line, feeling a little stupid now.

When finally, they entered the ice maze, she glanced dubiously at the ten foot walls of ice and did a rough calculation in her head of the approximate square footage.

It had to be at least five thousand square feet.

Once they were inside, it would be almost impossible to continue her hunt for her mystery notebook guy - unless he happened to be directly in front of her in the maze.

As she and Riley headed off down the first corridor, they had two choices; right or left.

Ally peered down each of the options, trying to gauge which was correct and which would lead into a dead end. There was no way to tell. And she didn't like the odds.

"Let's go this way, Aunt Ally," Riley chose the left without any thought.

But Ally was frustrated. If she had her phone, she could've grabbed an aerial view of their current location, focused in on the ice structure, downloaded the data into a GPS and then programmed it to find the quickest route possible to the exit.

They'd be in and out in no time.

But without GPS, this was going to take forever. And if they got lost, there was no way to call for help either!

She broke out in palpitations a little at the thought of being without her trusty phone, until Riley tugged on her jacket. "Come on! It's this way."

Ally forced herself to smile through her panic; this little guy was depending on her.

He took off running and Ally caught him at the next fork, just as he was turning left. She figured this was taking them backwards though, and he was most certainly heading in the wrong direction.

"Riley? I think we went the wrong way."

Laugher filled the ice passage, as he once again turned left, causing Ally to lose all sense of direction.

"Think we're lost?" he teased.

"I know we are." This made Riley laugh

even harder as he took off once again, taunting her to catch him.

And despite herself, and for the first time since she'd got here, Ally began to forget about her missing suitcase, and actually have some fun.

CHAPTER 14

*J*ake sat in the car with his sister, feeling like a couple of detectives on a stakeout as they watched everyone enter and exit the ice maze from the parking lot.

At least they knew what Ally's friend Lara looked like, given she had so many pictures on her social media profile.

But most importantly they'd garnered from her post that she'd be here this morning with her businesswoman friend, who presumably had Jake's case.

Despite this very promising lead, he still couldn't relax - at least not until they'd successfully located the woman and gotten his luggage back.

"You know, I still can't take you seriously, dressed like that," Meghan commented, with a snicker.

Jake looked down at the outfit he'd borrowed from his father. The clothes, while old-fashioned were warm and perfectly suited for the circumstances. Ice mazes by their nature were … icy cold.

And why his sister was focused on something so irrelevant when there was so much at stake here, was beyond him.

As they approached the entrance to the maze, the line was already stretching halfway to the parking lot.

Jake watched a small boy, patiently waiting in line holding his mother's hand. It reminded him of the very first time he'd come to this place as a child.

He could feel the kid's excitement as he marvelled at the ten foot walls made entirely of ice. Probably wondering how anyone could create such a thing, just like Jake had.

For the next few minute, he and Meghan continued to scan through everyone entering and exiting, hoping they'd be able to spot Ally's friend.

As they did so, Jake's gaze suddenly stopped on a woman with sleek mid-length brown hair.

He studied her profile, trying to figure out why she looked so familiar. Then he realised - it was the woman on the flight here, the one who didn't have any cash on her.

"Jake," his sister's voice brought him back to the present. "Why are you staring? That woman looks nothing like Lara."

"Uh I know." He looked back to where the woman from the flight was standing, to see her grab a young boy by the hand and smile down at him.

Oh she was a mom. For some reason he hadn't pictured her that way on the plane. At all.

"Look, look, I think that could be her!" Meghan exclaimed then, grabbing her brother by the arm.

He turned quickly as his sister pointed out a blond woman fitting Lara Clark's description, pushing a stroller back through the crowds at a very fast pace, only about a couple of feet away.

As he tried to follow, he did his best to

avoid bumping into all the people who were headed in the opposite direction.

"Sorry," he apologised, colliding with someone, then turned once the man assured him he was fine, only to come inches from running right into someone else.

Jake felt like a complete jerk; this wasn't him. He stopped, took a deep breath and looked once again to see how far away he was from reaching Ally Walker's friend.

But she was now at the door of her mini van, effortlessly lifting her baby's car seat in, folding down the stroller and speeding away.

Clearly this Lara had somewhere to be other than the ice maze. Was there some emergency with the baby that she had to leave?

And where was her friend? Was Ally already inside? Should he maybe go inside and search?

But neither he or Meghan had any idea what she looked like….

Frustrated afresh, he resisted the urge to fall to his knees. He'd been so close too.

The idea that if he had just been fast enough to reach that woman, he might well be holding his bag right now was enough to make him want to kick himself.

And the fact that he, a writer, was considering such a cliche made him even more annoyed.

"I just can't believe we just missed her," he groaned to Meghan.

Now it felt like he was right back at square one.

Not to mention that in the meantime, there was still no return call from the airline and without his precious notebook, no way for him to finish plotting out his next book in time.

To say nothing of the most pressing loss of all.

Heidi...

Tomorrow was Christmas Eve, and this situation truly was going from bad to worse.

CHAPTER 15

*H*aving changed Charlotte and taken the opportunity to grab a peaceful gingerbread latte while her son and Ally were in the maze, Lara returned to the parking lot, deciding to wait for them at the exit.

There was no point in dragging the baby in there now, not when she was already ornery after her diaper accident.

And knowing Ally, they would surely have made it out by now.

Sure enough, within a few minutes, the two came running through the exit.

"We made it!" Ally cried with some relief, when Lara drove over to meet them.

"See I told you!" Riley said proudly.

"Mommy, you should have seen it in there. It was so hard, but I found the way. It was so much fun."

"So glad you guys enjoyed it."

"I never would have made it without you," Ally laughed and the two high-fived each other as they got back into the car.

"So, any sign of green trousers guy?" Lara asked her then.

"Nope. The man you pointed out wasn't him and I didn't see anyone else fitting that description inside. It was a long shot but ..."

"Well, we can keep an eye out at the tree-lighting ceremony later. And ... wait!" Lara added, her eyes widening suddenly. The gala. You said there was a tux in there?"

The tux - of *course!* The guy surely wouldn't have packed a tuxedo unless he was going to The Snow Ball.

Ally felt her spirits lift, as she realised that if all else failed, maybe, just maybe, she had a real shot at finding J.T. Turner.

CHAPTER 16

That afternoon Lara baked peppermint fudge in the kitchen while Ally and Reilly made paper snowflakes by warmth of the fireplace, soft carols playing in the living room.

Through spending time with them all, Ally was beginning to finally understand why people traveled such great distances to enjoy the holidays with their families for the holidays.

It was so cosy and festive, it was almost enough to make her forget all about her conference calls scheduled for later that evening.

Almost.

She managed to get through them on Lara's rickety old wifi, but must to her friend's regret, the timing meant that she had to miss the tree-lighting ceremony.

While normally Ally would've jumped at the chance to forgo such a cheesy outing, she was now kinda sorry she'd scheduled any work stuff at all, she was enjoying herself so much.

Maybe now she could also understand why Mel had gone AWOL - clearly her assistant, unlike Ally, was able to leave the office behind.

But it meant that with Lara's family partaking in more festivities, she had the cosy house all to herself, and feeling a little stuffed after all the hot chocolate and peppermint fudge, from earlier, went upstairs to read more of the book, while awaiting the others' return.

In truth, the story had really grabbed her now, and she'd fallen a little bit in love with J.T. Turner's writing, especially the way he seemed so emotionally intuitive and interested in his characters.

Author or not, it kind of made her want to meet the owner of the suitcase all the more, and when Ally eventually reached the final page, she instinctively went to the case and idly looked through it again.

Weirdly drawn to feeling some way closer to the man who'd also been reading the same heartfelt words.

Then, suddenly conscious of how stalkerish it was, she deftly began zipping back up all the pockets, as if to hide evidence of her snooping.

But on one of the outside pockets (the one where she usually kept her phone charger) the zipper seemed strained.

Ally reached into the pocket to see if she could push the bulky object blocking it out of the way. Rummaging further inside, her fingers brushed up against something hard, yet velvety to the touch and curious afresh, she pulled it out.

To discover that it was a small navy blue box - a jewelry box.

Eyes widening, she tentatively opened the lid and sure enough, inside was a stunningly beautiful diamond ring.

An engagement ring…

For reasons that she couldn't quite explain, Ally's heart sank to the pit of her stomach.

The guy was obviously planning to propose to someone this Christmas.

And the realisation struck Ally then, that she really needed to get this bag back to its owner - for more reasons than one.

CHAPTER 17

*A*s he sat with his family over dinner after the tree lighting ceremony, Jake had a fresh spring in his step.

Finally, he had a lead - a proper lead!

Despite multiple calls to the airline subsequently, he'd heard nothing at all, and after missing Ally Walker's friend at the ice maze, was seriously beginning to give up all hope of getting his bag back.

Until on the way back from the maze, he'd popped in the general store, before joining Meghan for a hot chocolate at the cafe next door.

He knew he'd go out of his mind between now and Christmas trying to figure out a way to locate his bag - and the ring - and needed to distract himself.

What better way to do that than bury himself in his writing? To say nothing of the fact that he needed to finish plotting out the new book.

So, deciding to pick up a replacement note-book from the collection he knew they carried at the general store, he chatted briefly to the friendly owner.

"Must be something in the air today, Jake," Harry the owner commented, when he placed his purchase on the countertop to pay. "That's the second one I sold today, and you're usually my best customer for these."

"You mean, only customer." He nodded distractedly, not exactly in the mood for small talk until Harry said something else. "And there was a woman in earlier too, asking if anyone had bought one."

At this Jake's ears picked up, his author brain whirring instinctively. "Seems like an odd query."

"I thought the same. You know these out of towners though, strange as they come."

Jake smiled and was about to put his wallet

away when Harry's next words stopped him in his tracks.

"Wanted a charger for some futuristic phone she had - never seen anything like it."

The phone charger... the unusual one from Ally Walter's bag that even Meghan didn't recognise.

"Did she say anything about losing a charger along with her luggage?" he asked, and Harry looked up at him, surprised.

"Yes, as it happens. Some problem with the airline. Said all she had left was a dress for the Snow Ball tomorrow night."

The shoes .... suddenly all the pieces were clicking into place.

"What else did she say?" Jake pressed, thanking the heavens for small-town gossip, as Harry told him everything he could glean about the woman he was trying to find.

But most important of all, Ally Walters was heading to tomorrow night's gala.

So all Jake had to do now was arrange to connect with her at the Snow Ball, swap the bags back, and be reunited with his luggage - and the ring.

Now, as he looked across the dinner table at Heidi's pretty face shining in the candlelight, he finally allowed himself to relax.

Just in time.

CHAPTER 18

*O*n Christmas Eve, once the kids were
asleep, Ally and Lara went upstairs
to the master bedroom to get ready for the gala
ball.

The size of the bathroom was about the
same as her entire Boston apartment.

She watched as Lara looped large strands of
her hair around the barrel of her curling iron.
As she let them go, they fell into perfect rings.

"So are you excited about tonight?" her
friend asked.

Earlier that day, Lara had gotten a call from
the general store owner, passing on a message
from the owner of the bag, who'd somehow
managed to track her down.

They'd made arrangements to switch the cases back at tonight's event, and while Ally knew she should be thrilled about getting her stuff back, for some reason she felt ... flat.

It meant that J.T. would be reunited with the ring and get to propose to some lucky woman this Christmas, while she, Ally would be reunited with ... her phone charger.

"Ally, do you have a crush on this guy?" Lara's questions automatically made her cheeks redden. She looked down at the hairbrush in her hands, afraid her expression would invite even more questioning.

"What? No. Nothing like that. At all. I think maybe I've just built up a picture of him from his stuff and his writing. He just seems so ... intuitive."

As soon as the words were out of her mouth, she realised how foolish they sounded.

"I knew it! Oh this could really be the start of something you know. Maybe he's done the same with your stuff and tonight, will take one look at you and think losing his suitcase was the best thing that ever happened to him. So let's finish getting ready and get you to your Prince Charming."

Ally didn't have the heart to tell her about the ring, to say nothing of the fact that she didn't want to admit she'd been prying in the bag to that extent.

Better to let her idealistic friend enjoy her fantasy, nice and all as it was.

Lara put down the curling iron and Ally shook her head, watching her shiny curls bounce. It was exactly how her mother used to do her hair every Christmas Eve when she was a child.

She went back to her room and lifted the sparkling dress off of the hanger. Then held her breath as she slipped it on, hoping it still fit after four years waiting.

After struggling with the zipper a little, Ally went to the mirror and barely recognised her own reflection.

"Here we come! Get your cameras ready," Lara called to her husband, as Ally stood at the top of their huge staircase.

"Wow! You look … incredible. Doesn't she look great Mark?" Lara said proudly.

She and her husband looked like proud parents standing at the bottom of the staircase as Ally descended past the twinkling Christmas tree, feeling herself almost like a fairy princess.

She smiled, doing her best to join in the excitement and despite herself, couldn't help but wonder what J.T. might say when they finally met and he caught sight of her in this dress.

Then she kicked herself for thinking the guy would say anything other than, 'thanks for my suitcase.'

Lara and her silly, romantic notions were well and truly starting to get to her.

CHAPTER 19

When her friend had told Ally that Mark's family ran the town inn, she'd pictured a small bed and breakfast, maybe converted from an existing large old home with a few guest rooms.

She couldn't have imagined they in fact owned a full scale hotel, with eighteen bedrooms, a fine dining restaurant, plus a ballroom big enough to hold the entire town's population.

"This is … incredible," Ally gushed, as she climbed the massive centre staircase that lead from the lobby to the ballroom, fully bedecked in sparkling holiday finest.

Holding the hem of her dress with one

hand to prevent herself from tripping, she took a quick peek to see if the shoes she had borrowed were visible as she walked.

It was kind of Lara to lend her some heels since her own were still in her bag. Though these were a bit big for her and she could already feel blisters forming on the backs of her heels.

The three made their way through the crowd at a snail's pace, stopping to talk with a few of Mark and Lara's friends.

Everyone was very cordial and polite to her, an out of towner, but once they had asked Ally an appropriate number of questions about her career and Boston, the conversation would once again turn to community or children.

And once again Ally felt herself at a loss, beginning to realise that her life was totally defined by work. She didn't belong here, and the realisation made her sad.

J.T had requested to meet at the top of the staircase at 9pm. Which was only a few minutes from now.

Ally was eager and nervous all at the same time. Though once the exchange was final, at least she'd be free to head home and put herself out of her misery.

"Hey, it's almost 9pm," Lara said then, touching her arm gently. "Are you sure you don't want Mark to just meet the guy and switch back the bags?"

"Thanks but no, I'm fine." Ally couldn't quite put her finger on it.

But for some reason this felt personal.

SHE MADE her way back out front, where there was a small table and friendly volunteers that checked everyone's tickets.

They had been kind enough to watch the suitcase and Ally did her best to smile as she grabbed it and headed back up the staircase to the meeting spot.

Feeling unaccountably alone, she just hoped he would be punctual so they could get this over and done with.

And instinctively reached into her purse to check the exact time on her phone, feeling silly yet again for relying on it when it was long dead.

She looked around and spotted a grandfather clock at the top of the stairs whereupon a loud chime announced 9pm exactly.

"Ally?" The voice from the bottom of the stairs made her breath catch in her throat a little.

And as her gaze moved down the stairs to the marble tile of the lobby floor, the first thing she spotted was her case.

The slightly worn wheels, the wonky top zipper ... how had she not noticed at the time that the other one was far too pristine to be hers?

The man holding her own picked it up in one hand and began climbing the stairs. As he climbed higher, Ally noticed first what a nice tux he had on. Obviously must've found a replacement somewhere.

And next, that Lara was wrong about J.T. being an old man.

In fact he seemed to be about the same age as she.

It was only in that moment that it finally registered; he'd called her by name. How on earth did he know her name?

Ally finally looked up at his face, and the

instant she looked into his blue-green eyes, she couldn't believe it.

The guy from the flight … The plaid sports coat, the water, him jokingly reading his book - all the memories of that brief encounter suddenly came rushing back.

"It's … you," she gasped.

CHAPTER 20

*B*ut still, how on earth did he know her name?

Then Ally felt silly, realising that she'd forgotten her business card was attached to the handle.

Which meant that it should've been easy for him to reach her before now?

But of course, she remembered then, her phone was long dead and Mel had since disappeared into the festive ether.

So how *did* he find her?

"Jake," he greeted, extending a hand. "Nice to meet you - again."

"I can't ... believe it was you all along." For some reason she felt completely tongue-tied.

"I'm so sorry I picked up your stuff by mistake. I'm sure you've missed this." He gestured towards her bag.

"I have. And same with you." She went to hand the other case to him then, then hesitated. "Actually I'm not a hundred percent sure this is yours, though. I think it belongs to a writer named J.T."

He laughed, and she wondered what he could possibly find funny about all this.

"J.T. is my author name. I take it you found my books ... and my notebook? At least I hope that's still there." He grimaced.

OK, maybe that made sense.

"It is. And don't worry; all your stuff is still inside. Although I should admit I did read a book. Sorry about that."

"Don't be. In fact, if you want to keep it, I have plenty."

Jake took his suitcase and lightly patted the outer pocket while Ally did her best to not feel a little offended.

Or deflated.

"Don't worry, the ring is still there, too."

He exhaled. "Man, you have no idea what a relief that is! My brother would've killed me."

Brother … Her mind froze as she stopped to think what this meant. The ring belonged to his brother?

"He's planning on proposing to his girl-friend, Heidi tomorrow morning. I offered to pick up the ring at the family jeweler in Boston on the way here. To be honest, I didn't even tell him my bag was missing, but I was beginning to really worry I wouldn't find you in time."

"How did you find me?" she asked, genuinely curious.

"Well, my sister found your social media profile and we went to seek you out with your friend at the ice maze yesterday. And believe it or not, I even saw you standing in line - with a little kid."

"You saw me with Riley? But why didn't you come up and talk to us? He's Lara's son." She couldn't believe it. "Especially when I was looking for you there too. The guy at the store said…"

"Exactly. I couldn't believe it when he told me that a woman had been in looking for a charger and asking if anyone had bought a notebook. I knew it had to be you. Well, not that I knew that it was actually *you*, in that you are Ally. But I'm so glad it is."

Her eyes flickered upward, and her heart began to speed up. "You are?"

He smiled, eyes twinkling. "Yes. And I'm not sure if you've realised this yet, but this is pretty much a tech-free town. Cash only. So if you need someone to buy you a drink …"

Ally winced a little.

"Aw I'm sorry, I guess I shouldn't have assumed," Jake said quickly, colouring.

"No, I just need to change my shoes," she admitted, reddening too. "My feet are *killing* me. I had to borrow these from my friend and they're way too small."

She shifted from one foot to the other, trying to minimize her discomfort, while also trying to process what exactly was going on here.

The guy from the plane was J.T.

Jake.

"I'm sorry it took me so long to find you," he was saying, while Ally did her best to squat down low enough in her dress to unzip her suitcase.

She tottered a little and almost fell backwards toward the stairs, but Jake put a hand out to steady her.

"Let me."

He unzipped her bag for her, knowing the shoes were right on top.

Ally happily kicked off Lara's torturous heels, and awkwardly tried to balance on one foot as Jake set hers on the floor in front of her.

Then incredibly, he crouched down and steadied her with one hand, while using the other to hold up a shoe for her to place her foot inside.

Ally felt dizzy.

"Better?" he grinned once both sparkly sandals were duly fastened on her feet.

"So much."

Then Jake gallantly extended his elbow and Ally smiled, feeling a little like Cinderella as she placed her arm inside it.

And with the ring now safely in his inside pocket, Jake and Ally stowed their cases, and together set off back to the ballroom.

CHAPTER 21

*J*ust as they were halfway across the dance floor and heading for the bar, the lights turned low.

"Time to find that special someone and make your way onto the floor," the singer of the band announced as the opening bars of *A Lot Like Christmas* began to play.

Ally stood frozen with awkwardness, while all around men took their partners and wives by the hand.

Turning to Jake, she was certain he felt the same discomfort, but when her gaze met his, she saw him smile.

"Talk about timing. Shall we?" He gently took Ally's right hand and placed it on top of his shoulder, then took the other and placed it on his side, before wrapping his own around her waist.

Her arms felt rigid as wooden boards. What must everyone be thinking?

She looked around the room, feeling reassured then that absolutely no one else was even looking in their direction. They were all too busy with their own dance partners. So she began to relax a little and enjoy the moment.

Ally and Jake began to move slowly to the music, their bodies finding a natural pace within seconds.

Then over her shoulder she spotted Lara, whose eyes were out on stalks. She grinned and gave Ally a big thumbs up before placing her head back onto Mark's shoulder.

Copying her example, Ally did the same.

As soon as her head found a comfortable position on Jake's shoulder, a sense of almost surreal calm descended upon her. Following his lead felt so natural that she was able to completely lose herself in the moment.

And in his arms.

They continued to dance for what seemed

like hours, until eventually Lara tapped her on the shoulder.

"So sorry to interrupt you two, but we really should get going. I promised the sitter."

"Oh! I totally lost track of time."

Jake stood back and still smiling, he grabbed her hand and kissed it.

"See you the day after tomorrow? I'll text you the address - now that you've got your charger back. And Merry Christmas."

Ally nodded, and once she'd collected her case and they headed back to the car, Lara could hardly wait to hear all the details.

"The day after tomorrow?" she urged. "Tell me everything!"

"Yes, Jake - J.T. - invited me to dinner with his family. And his brother's engagement celebrations."

"Amazing!" Her friend hugged her. "You guys look so perfect together. And he seems wonderful. But I thought you were leaving for Florida the day after tomorrow?"

"I think I might stay on a while longer if that's OK with you?"

"Of course - as long as you like!"

Ally smiled as gently falling snowflakes

cooled her rosy cheeks. This truly was turning out to be the strangest, but perhaps the best, Christmas yet.

And she got the sense that from now on - in more ways than one - maybe she wouldn't need to travel light.

Enjoyed this novella?

Read on for an excerpt of another of Melissa Hill's heartwarming festive reads 12 Dogs of Christmas, available now in ebook and paperback.

12 DOGS OF CHRISTMAS

Animal lover Lucy feels blessed with her dream job; walking other people's dogs for a living. The pooches she cares for are her closest friends - as good as family, and Lucy would concede that she certainly understands them a lot more than people.

She wouldn't admit to having favourites among her charges, but if she really had to choose, it would be Berry; a huge, fun-loving Labradane who never stops eating. One day, when dropping Berry back to his elderly owner, Lucy is immediately concerned when there's no reply. Until a neighbour breaks the news that sadly the old woman has died.

And when absent relatives quickly make it clear that the dog is not their problem, Lucy realises she's the only one left to take care of Berry.

Her landlord won't let her take him in - even temporarily - so in order to help the big dog find a home in time for the holidays, Lucy needs to push herself out of her comfort zone and into the community in her quest to find Berry his perfect match.

Soon realising that sometimes it's not just dogs but people, who need rescuing too.

CHAPTER 1

The curtains were wide open when Lucy Adams woke up. She must have forgotten to close them the night before, and now she was glad for that.

Snow outlined the windowsill like a frame, and the blanketed San Juan Mountains - the sun just peeking above its summit - was the picture.

It was a beautiful sight to wake up to.

She sighed happily. Small town life was very different to what it had been like in Denver, but she should have known the city wasn't for her.

Lucy was a Whitedale native, born and bred.

Once upon a time, she thought that time in the big city would help her shyness, and allow her to live out her grandmother's dream of her becoming a success.

Gran had been so sure that Lucy becoming an investigative journalist and seeing her name on the by-line of a story would have spurred her on to even greater things, but it didn't.

Because she never got any further than being a fact-checker.

Lucy was cripplingly shy; always had been. When she was a child her mother tried everything to help bring her out of her shell, but it was no use.

Her timidity and innate reserve around people made it difficult for her to even broach the subject of an article to her boss.

In the end, she realized that no matter how hard she tried, she'd never be as happy in Denver as she would be back home.

So home she came.

Now, she swung her legs from beneath the sheets and did a few quick stretches to loosen herself up for the day ahead. Then quickly made her bed; the wrinkled sheets and pillow depressed on only one side.

Her apartment was the best she could afford; a small upper-level two-bed on Maypole Avenue, close to all the parks and trails.

When she started renting it a couple of years ago, she'd sort of hoped that by now she'd have someone to share it with, but no such luck.

Lucy didn't know why, but she seemed to have been born without the romance gene too.

She knew she wasn't bad looking, with her shoulder-length caramel-colored hair and fair skin. Her smile was big and warm, but the problem likely was that she didn't really smile around people.

Animals yes; humans not so much.

People made her nervous, which was why having a dog-walking business was a plus. Lucy spent her days surrounded entirely by those who understood her without judgment.

Lucy was very proud of her business, 12 Dogs Walking Service. It was the premier dog-walking outfit in town, and she had dreams of making it even better.

Once she had enough money saved and found the right location, she fully intended to add other services, like doggie daycare and pet pampering.

She envisioned her little business as one day being the best animal care center in the county, if not the state.

But hey, one day at a time.

THE WOODEN FLOORS were cool beneath her feet as Lucy left her bedroom and walked into the kitchen.

She fixed herself a bowl of cereal and a cup of coffee while waiting for her computer to wake.

She loved her trusty old-model Dell PC, but Betsy was on her last legs. It used to take less than a minute for it to boot up, now it was more like seven.

Lucy hummed the lyrics to *Must Have Been the Mistletoe* as she got out her apple cinnamon granola and almond milk. She did her best to eat well, and in Whitedale that was made easier by the popularity of the farm-to-table movement.

Then she settled at her two-seater dining

table by the small window overlooking the square.

The town was slowly coming to life - in a few hours, cars and people would be bustling along the streets, but for the moment it was just store owners looking for an early start, and a few joggers out for a morning run.

When the PC was fully loaded, the home screen flickered to life, and a picture of a golden-haired cocker spaniel greeted Lucy, making her smile immediately.

"So let's see what's going on today..." she mumbled as she opened her emails; a couple of subscription updates to animal magazines and journals, and a few more notifying her of pet trade shows in the area.

Then requests from her clients.

Bob St. John wanted Blunders walked on Thursday. He was a new client and Blunders, a three-year-old dachshund, was sorely in need of Lucy's services.

Bob, loving owner that he was, had been won over by Blunder's pleading looks, and now the dog was carrying a little too much weight. The extra pounds for a larger breed might've been easier to handle, but the dachshund's long body made it more easily prone to herniated discs.

The sooner Blunders got the exercise in, and if Bob stuck to the diet the vet had recommended, Lucy was sure that the little dog would be fine in no time.

"Dear Bob …" she intoned out loud, as she began to type a response confirming the date and time, and set an alert reminder for herself on her phone.

Martha Bigsby wanted Charlie walked every day that week. Charlie was a six-year-old Airedale Terrier. His coat was perfect and thankfully so was his health. He was Martha's prize-winning pooch and she loved him dearly.

Lucy loved owners who shared her appreciation for their animals. Charlie had a big show coming up before the holidays, and she wanted to be sure he was ready for it.

Dear Martha. I confirm that I'll pick up Charlie at seven each morning this week. We can return to our normal nine o'clock slot once you're back from Bakersfield.

She spent the next twenty minutes replying

to her work emails before checking her personal ones, though was finished with those in less than one.

Lucy's life consisted mostly of work, and very little of the social aspects that most other people found entertaining. Socialising just wasn't her thing really.

She'd always been happier around animals than people. They, especially dogs, were easy to understand and predictable for the most part.

People weren't, and that was a difficulty for Lucy. She liked what she could rely on and she'd been disappointed far too many times by people.

Never by her furry friends.

Her phone rang then and she checked the caller display. It was Eustacia, her neighbor on the floor below; a woman who believed it was her job to marry off every singleton in their building.

"Lucy? Are you there? Of course, you're there. You're screening my calls aren't you?" Eustacia's Brooklyn accent pierced her ears.

Her new neighbor, who had moved from New York four months ago, was convinced she knew what was best for Lucy, and that she'd find her the 'perfect guy'.

"Trust me. I know all about these things. At home, they used to call me the matchmaker. I can set up anyone with anyone. You leave it to me. A young girl like you shouldn't be all alone every night. It's ain't natural."

Lucy would've appreciated the help, if it weren't for the fact that Eustacia had terrible taste in men.

"Mrs. Abernathy in 4C told me that her son Martin is back in town. And I told her you'd love to meet him. Would you give her a call? She says he'd loved to meet you too."

A perfect example of Eustacia's poor taste: Martin Abernathy was four years older than Lucy. He had a habit of snorting all the time and when she was little, he used to stick gum in her hair.

She rolled her eyes as her neighbor's shrill voice continued. She washed the dishes and put them away, and Eustacia was *still* talking.

Then, finally making her excuses, Lucy hung up the phone and got ready for work.

Her clothing and shoes were comfortable,

cosy and most importantly, breathable. There was a *lot* of walking around in her line of work, and no matter what the deodorant companies claimed, she'd rather be safe than sorry.

Dogs were after all, very sensitive to smell.

CHAPTER 2

First, Lucy headed to Olympus Avenue, where one of her charges resided.

While the service was called 12 Dogs, in truth she rarely had as many pooches all at once, but could certainly handle that much.

She also didn't do favorites, and would never admit to having one. Much like people, breeds were individual, and to say you liked dog one better than the other was somewhat unfair. People couldn't help who they were and neither could animals.

However, if Lucy *truly* had to choose a favorite dog – and was absolutely pressed on the matter – she'd pick Berry Cole.

Berry was a five-year-old chocolate brown Labrador and Great Dane mix – a Labradane.

Lucy just called him a sweetie.

He was loyal and loving, and despite his humongous size, being closer in build to his Great Dane mother than his Lab father, he was very gentle.

He was also the perfect choice for his owner, Mrs Cole. Though Lucy sometimes wondered how the seventy-five-year-old woman managed to feed the colossus.

He was *always* hungry, so much so that Lucy had started carrying extra snacks soon after he'd joined her troop.

Though if she could pick a dog for herself, it couldn't be one as huge as Berry. But that was a moot point, because unfortunately, Lucy's landlord didn't allow pets in the building.

Mrs. Cole was a widow with no children, and Lucy sometimes wondered if that would be her own fate - a life alone.Though at least Mrs. Cole had a canine companion. She didn't even have that.

Now she knocked on the door.

"Morning," Mrs. Cole greeted Lucy with a

smile the moment she opened the door. She looked tired today, more so than on most mornings when she called to pick up Berry.

Maybe she was feeling down.

Lucy could bring her back something from Toasties to perk up her spirits. It was the best cafe and pastry store in all of Whitedale, and Mrs. Cole had a thing for their Peppermint Chocolate Croissants.

"Hi, Mrs. Cole. Is he ready?" The words came out in a plume of white. Winter was well and truly here and Christmas now only a couple of weeks away.

They'd had their first heavy snowfall just a few days before and soon, the entirety of Whitedale would be covered in it.

The words had only just left Lucy's mouth, when the big dog came bounding to the door. He rushed past his owner and promptly jumped up and landed his big paws on her chest, knocking her back a step.

"Berry, calm down," Mrs. Cole scolded lightly.

"It's okay," Lucy laughed as Berry licked her face. "He's just happy to see me."

The older woman chuckled. "He always is. I

can't contend with him like I used to with this hip. I'm so happy he still gets to go out and have fun when you're around."

"It's my pleasure, and you know I really love this big guy," Lucy chuckled as she removed his paws from her chest and stooped down to scratch behind his ears.

Mrs. Cole duly handed her the leash from by the door and Lucy clipped it in place. She carried spare leashes and clean-up items in her backpack, but it was important to get Berry on the right track from the get-go.

"He's staying out for the whole day, yes?" she confirmed.

"Yes, if that's good with you."

Mrs. Cole was one of the few people Lucy could chat easily to. She supposed it was because she reminded her so much of the grandmother who had raised her.

She didn't have anyone now though. A fact she was well used to, but whenever Christmas came around, it was just that little bit harder to bear.

"Of course. You have a great day," Lucy told Mrs Cole as she began to lead Berry from the porch. "And get back inside, it's cold out. We'll see you later."

"You too," the older woman called after her, chuckling as Lucy struggled to keep pace with the dog. "And don't let the big guy wear you out too much."

END OF EXCERPT

12 DOGS OF CHRISTMAS is out now in paperback and ebook.

ABOUT THE AUTHOR

International #1 and USA Today bestselling author Melissa Hill lives in County Wicklow, Ireland.

Her page-turning emotional stories of family, friendship and romance have been translated into 25 different languages and are regular chart-toppers internationally.

A Reese Witherspoon x Hello Sunshine adaptation of her bestseller SOMETHING FROM TIFFANY'S hits screens worldwide in Dec '22 via Prime Video.

THE CHARM BRACELET aired in 2020 as a holiday movie A Little Christmas Charm. A GIFT TO REMEMBER (and a sequel) was also adapted for screen by Hallmark Channel and multiple other titles by Melissa are currently in development for film and TV.

Visit her website at

www.melissahill.info
Or get in touch via social media links below.

Printed in Great Britain
by Amazon

11858280R00082